MW00982226

Too Many Suns
Julie Lawson
Martin Springett
Stoddart

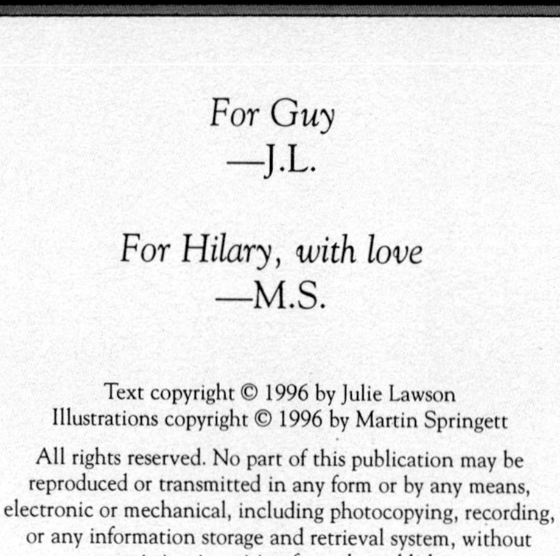

For Guy
—J.L.

For Hilary, with love
—M.S.

Martin Springett gives special thanks to Tony Watt, and is grateful to Jack Howard at the Far Eastern Library, the ROM.

Stoddart Publishing gratefully acknowledges the support of the Canada Council, Ontario Ministry of Citizenship, Culture and Recreation, Ontario Arts Council, and Ontario Publishing Centre in the development of writing and publishing in Canada.

First published in 1996 by
Stoddart Publishing Co. Limited
34 Lesmill Road
Toronto, Canada M3B 2T6
(416) 445-3333

In the United States contact
Stoddart Publishing Co. Limited
85 River Rock Drive, Unit 202
Buffalo, New York 14207, 1-800-805-1083

Canadian Cataloguing in Publication Data

Lawson, Julie, 1947–
Too many suns

ISBN 0-7737-2897-X
I. Springett, Martin. II. title.

PS 8573.A94T6 1995 jC813'.54 C95-930912-8
PZ7.L38To 1995

Printed and bound in Hong Kong

In a time when dragons were still young, on a farm shaded by mulberry trees, there lived ten brothers. Every morning at sunrise they would begin their day's work, from Eldest Brother on down.

All but Youngest Brother. He was up long before the others, greeting the dawn with more joy than the roosters, for Youngest Brother loved the sun.

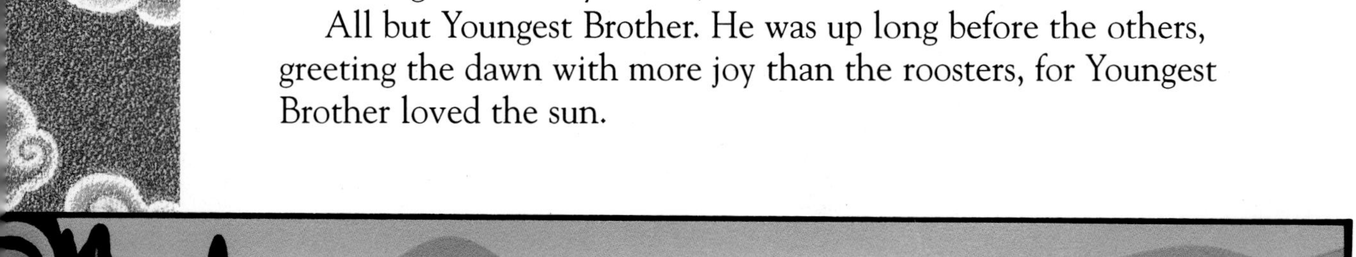

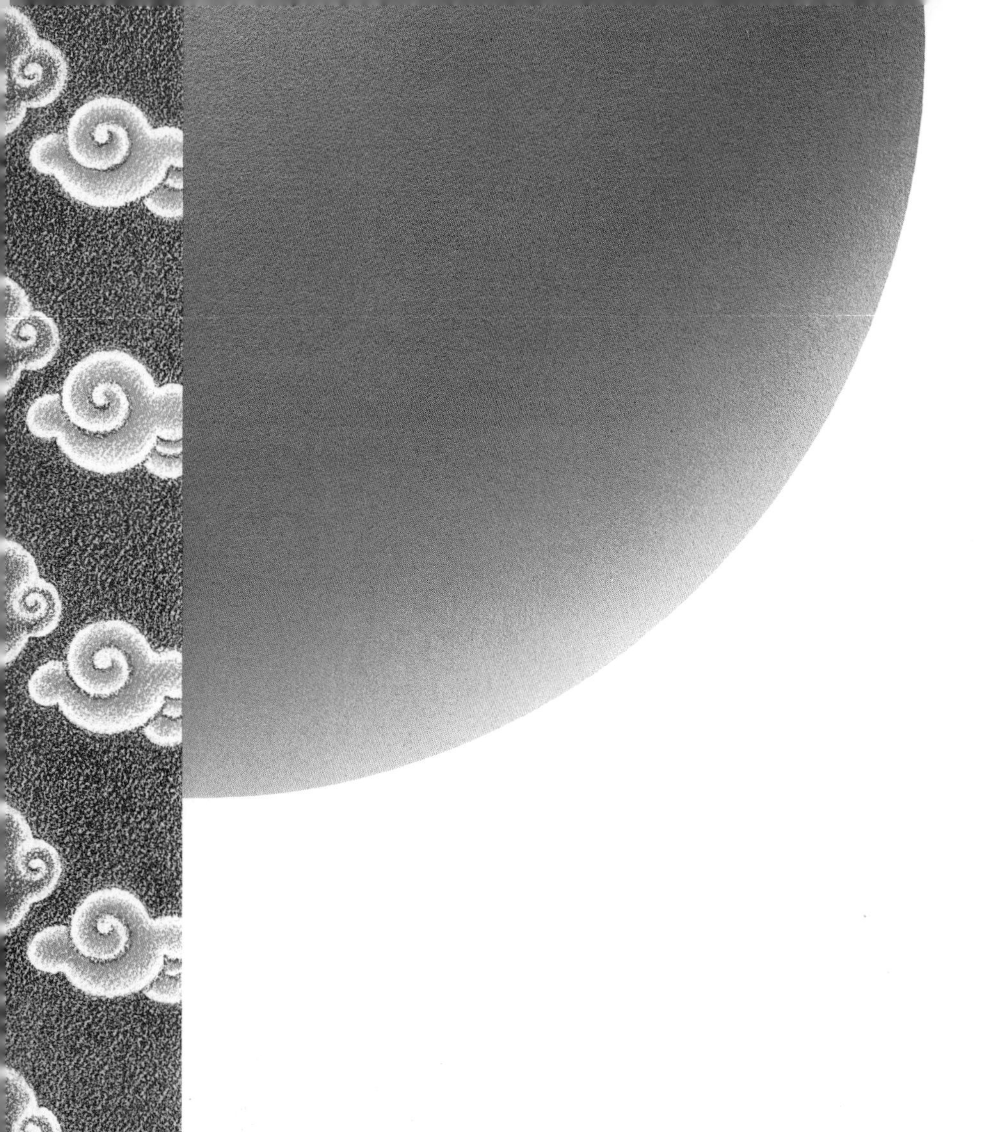

He loved the way it splashed the sky with crimson, the way it washed the rice shoots emerald-green, the way it streaked the river with gold. "One day," he vowed, "I will paint those colours. One day I will paint the sun."

Youngest Brother was a dreamer, but he always did his share of the work. He helped feed the chickens and ducks and pigs. He tended the water buffalo, ploughed the earth, and planted the rice seeds. Alongside his brothers, he flooded the fields and transplanted the seedlings. He weeded the rice paddies day after day, until harvest time.

Youngest Brother didn't mind helping. "This is the way of things," he said. "But one day, some day, I will paint the sun."

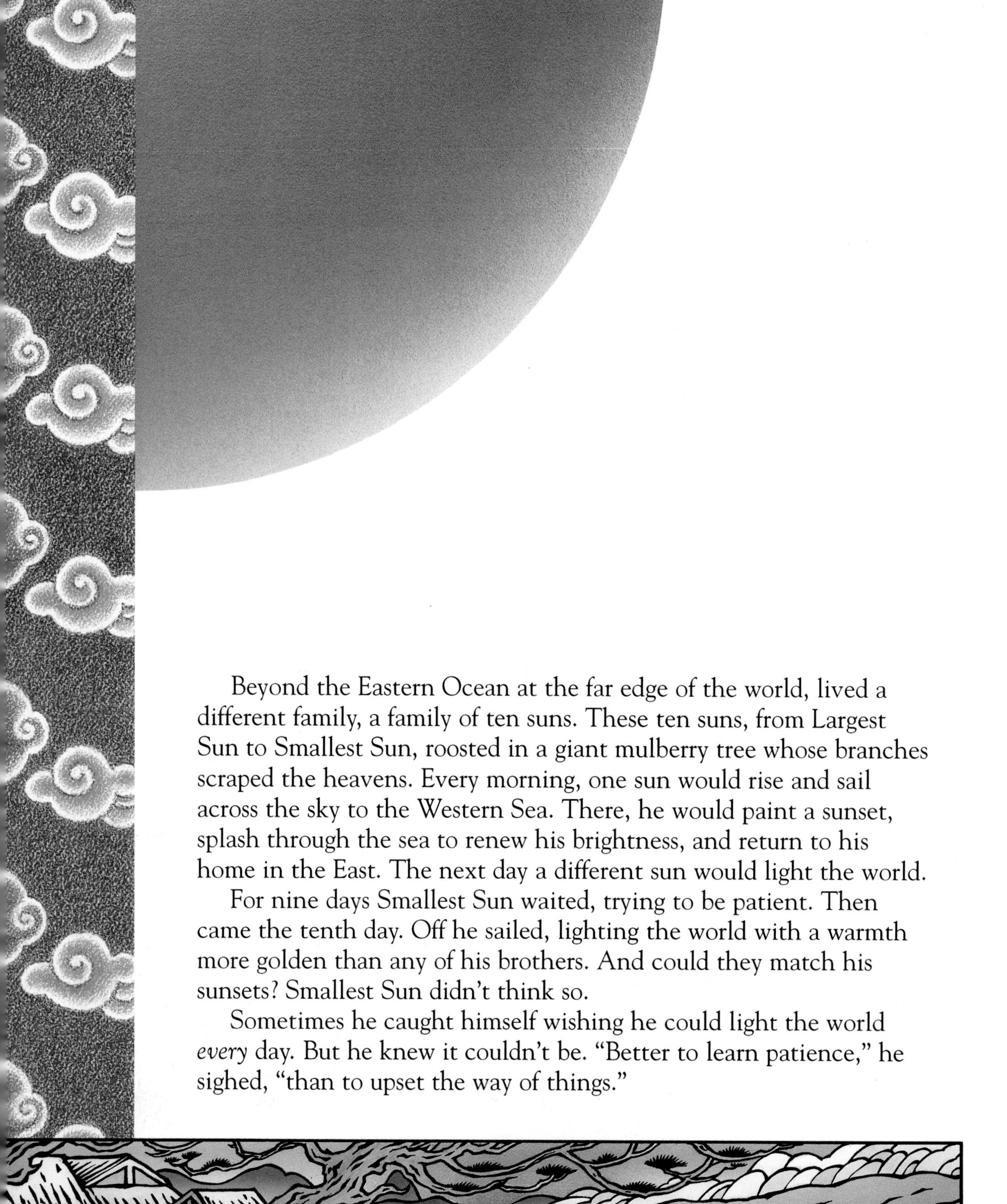

Beyond the Eastern Ocean at the far edge of the world, lived a different family, a family of ten suns. These ten suns, from Largest Sun to Smallest Sun, roosted in a giant mulberry tree whose branches scraped the heavens. Every morning, one sun would rise and sail across the sky to the Western Sea. There, he would paint a sunset, splash through the sea to renew his brightness, and return to his home in the East. The next day a different sun would light the world.

For nine days Smallest Sun waited, trying to be patient. Then came the tenth day. Off he sailed, lighting the world with a warmth more golden than any of his brothers. And could they match his sunsets? Smallest Sun didn't think so.

Sometimes he caught himself wishing he could light the world *every* day. But he knew it couldn't be. "Better to learn patience," he sighed, "than to upset the way of things."

On the Farm of Ten Brothers, life unfolded in a sunlit stream of days. Youngest Brother worked, cutting down the rice plants, collecting the stalks for drying and threshing, then ploughing the fields only to begin again, for this was the way of things.

But maybe it didn't have to be. Sometimes Youngest Brother thought his farm had too many brothers. Maybe when he was older, he would go his own way, choose a different path. Perhaps he would follow the path of the sun and paint it along the way. That thought made him work harder. Still, whenever he could, he stole a few moments in the sunshine.

"Go back to your chores," Eldest Brother scolded. But Youngest Brother was too busy playing hide and seek with his shadow to listen.

"Come on!" yelled Third Brother. "You'll fall behind in your weeding!"

"In a minute!" Youngest Brother answered. He couldn't stop now; he was racing the wind with his kite.

His nine brothers weren't really worried. This boy might be the youngest, but he worked as hard as the best of them. Besides, on a glorious day for kite flying, the weeds could wait.

"Don't blame us if there's no supper left," Middle Brother teased as they left the fields at the end of the day.

Youngest Brother paid no attention. Any minute now, the sun would set. If he was lucky, he might see the delicious shimmer of purple again, the one with a twist of tangerine. Now *there* was a colour to save for the day when he would paint the sun.

Time passed. Every tenth day, Smallest Sun dazzled the world with his sunsets. For nine days he rested in the branches of the mulberry tree, patiently waiting for his turn. And then, one day, his brothers decided to change things.

"Why do we have to take turns?" asked Largest Sun. "I hate spending nine days roosting like a bird in a tree."

Smallest Sun was surprised. He thought *he* was the impatient one.

"Yes, why?" echoed Fiery Sun. "Wouldn't the world enjoy more light and warmth?"

"Look at that young fellow down there," said Flaming Sun. "How he loves the sunshine! With more of us, his joy would be that much greater."

The suns clamoured with excitement. All but Smallest Sun. "What's wrong with you?" they asked.

Smallest Sun replied, "I don't like taking turns either, but isn't that the way of things?"

His brothers refused to answer.

Next morning the suns rose together. All but Smallest Sun.

"Don't be such a thundercloud," the nine suns teased. "Shine with us."

Reluctantly, Smallest Sun shone. It was his day after all. But his light was overshadowed by the blaze of his brothers.

It didn't take long for Smallest Sun to see that what they were

doing was wrong. The world did not enjoy ten times as much light and warmth. While his brothers raced each other across the sky, Smallest Sun watched Earth's frightened creatures, blinded by the light, scurrying for shelter. "Stop!" he cried. "We're going against the way of things!"

The suns paid no attention.

On the Farm of Ten Brothers, the mulberry trees stopped giving shade. Rice plants shrivelled, streams ran dry. Youngest Brother's kite lay limp on the ground, bleached to the colour of ashes. The ten brothers stood by helplessly as their animals weakened from thirst. Shielding their eyes from the glare, they shook their fists at the relentless suns.

Smallest Sun tried again. "We must take turns," he warned. "We're upsetting the way of things."

The suns still ignored him. Their light was so fierce, even the moon and stars remained hidden. "Splash into the Western Sea," Smallest Sun begged, "so night can come and cool the land."

But everyone was too busy chasing sunbeams to listen.

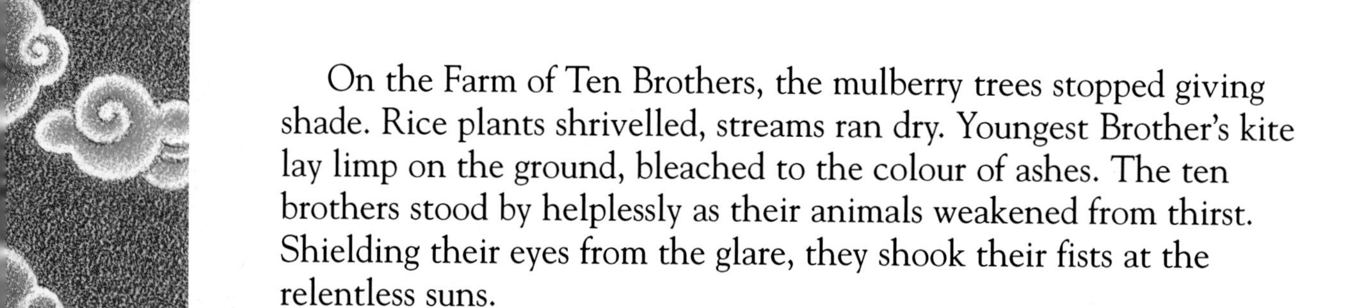

Before long, the Jade Emperor, sitting high in the Celestial Kingdom, felt an unusual heat rising up to warm his feet. He glanced down and saw the ten suns. Still farther down he could see the suffering they were causing. "This reckless behaviour must be stopped!" he fumed.

But what could he do? Like Smallest Sun, the Jade Emperor begged and pleaded. He reasoned and threatened. Finally, he sent for Yi, the Immortal Archer. "I've tried everything," he said. "You'll have to go to Earth and put an end to this havoc. Take your magical bow and arrows and shoot down the suns."

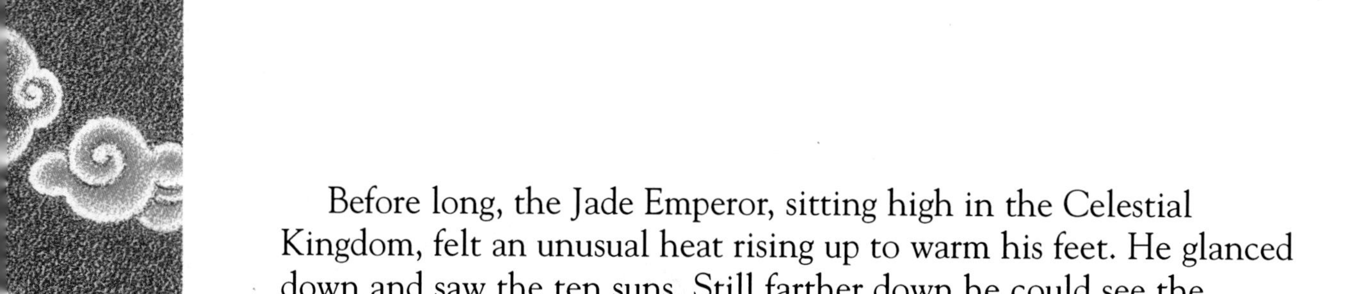

Yi bravely accepted the challenge. He rode off on the wind, leaving the Celestial Kingdom far behind.

Only Smallest Sun noticed him pass. "The Immortal Archer is about. He will shoot us down. We must go home, before it's too late."

But the suns were too busy painting the sky with dragons, cloud-breathing dragons that mocked the world with their empty promise of rain.

When Yi reached Earth, his heart was moved by the suffering of the people. He strode to the top of the highest mountain, faced the ten suns and thundered, “You have one last chance!” He raised his bow as a warning.

But the suns were too busy spinning cartwheels to notice. All but Smallest Sun. Stealthily, he crept toward the West.

“Very well then,” Yi said. Fitting an arrow to his bow, he took careful aim and fired. *Zing!* The arrow pierced the heart of Largest Sun. Down he plunged, a flaming ball of fire.

Smallest Sun crept closer to the Western Sea.

Zing! Again and again Yi's arrows found their mark. The suns fell smouldering to the ground.

Little by little the world began to breathe. Swirls of cloud promised rain. A coolness like deep green jade lightened the hearts of everyone on the Farm of Ten Brothers. "With a few days of rain the fields will be restored," they said hopefully.

Finally, one arrow remained for the last sun far to the West. Smallest Sun looked at Yi in dismay. He had almost reached the safety of the Western Sea. With colourful rays, he pleaded for his life.

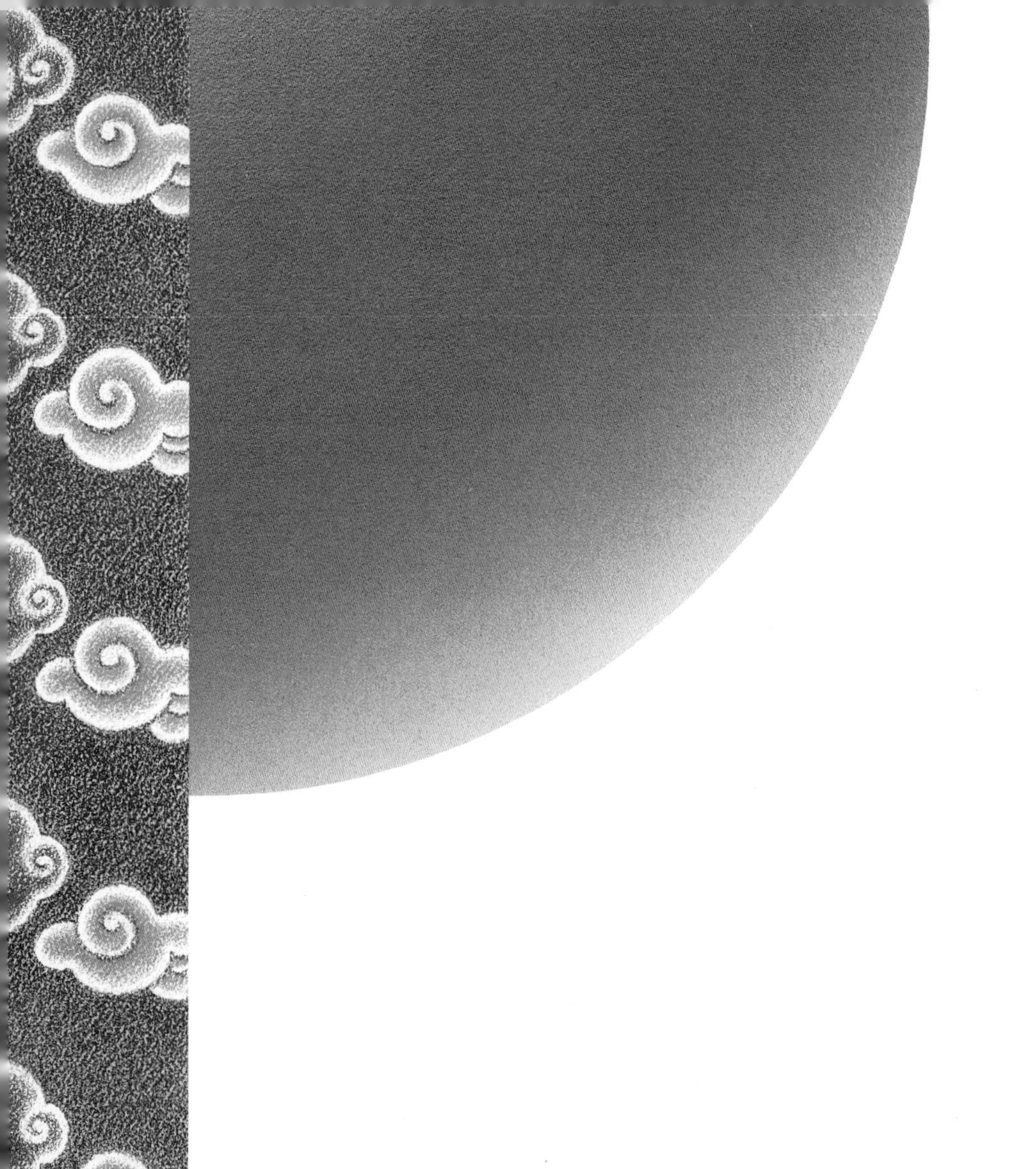

Youngest Brother watched Yi the Archer reach into his quiver for the arrow. Panic seized him. What if this sun were shot? No sun at all would be as terrible as too many suns. How could rice grow without light? How could anything live without warmth? How could he paint the sun if it vanished?

Shaking off his weariness, he raced up the mountain toward the Archer and tugged the loose folds of Yi's robe. Unaware, Yi fitted his arrow against the bowstring. Youngest Brother tugged harder. Yi glanced down and saw the boy reaching up to him.

Youngest Brother swallowed hard. Gathering up his courage he begged, "Please! Leave us one sun."

With a jolt, the Immortal Archer realized just what he was about to do. "You are right," he said, lowering his arrow. "One sun must remain." Together, he and Youngest Brother watched Smallest Sun dip silently into the Western Sea.

From that time on there has only been one sun to light the world. This has become the way of things. True to his dreams, Youngest Brother left the farm and followed the path of the sun. Along the way he painted its colours, from the shimmer of purple to the arrow-sharp twist of tangerine.

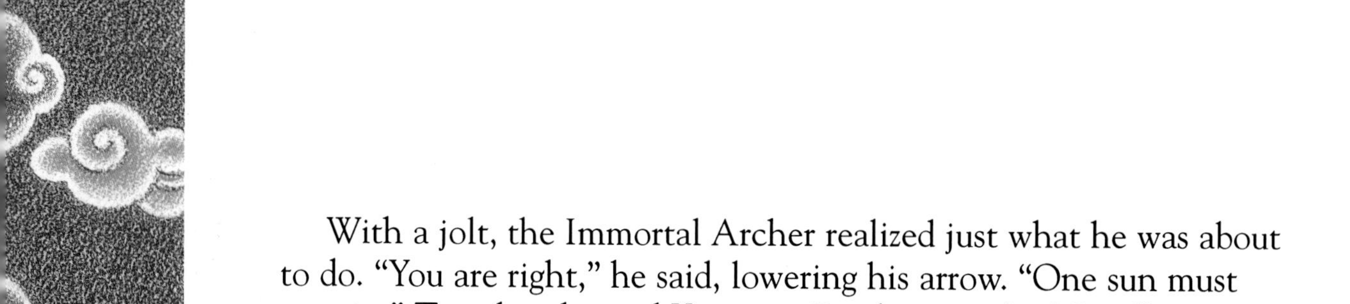

Author's Note

From the most ancient times, the sun has been an important symbol in Chinese mythology. It was considered the essence of the *yang*, or male principle, in nature, and the source of all brightness. The sun was also a symbol of the Emperor.

At one time, it was believed that ten suns ruled the world. One early literary source says that the suns were carried by birds. Another claims that these birds, red crows with three legs, were inside the suns. Whatever the case, it is not surprising that ancient people, living in a land where drought was all too common, believed in the existence of multiple suns.

According to stories surrounding this legend, each time Yi, the Immortal Archer, shot one of the suns, a ball of fire exploded in the air and a huge three-legged crow fell to Earth. As for the fireballs, they fell into the Eastern Sea and formed a gigantic rock so hot that the waters touching it instantly evaporated. Thus, even though all rivers and streams empty into it, the sea itself never overflows.

When his task was accomplished, Yi chose to remain on Earth as a mortal. For some time he lived happily with his wife, Chang E, but eventually, fearing death, he longed to regain his status as a god. Through heroic deeds, he succeeded in obtaining the Elixir of Immortality. Clearly he intended to drink it, but there are different versions of what happened next.

In one, Chang E, also thirsting for immortality, steals the elixir from her husband. She flees to the moon for safety, but is changed into a toad for her greediness. Sometimes the outline of this toad can be seen in the moon's surface.

In another version, Yi is murdered before he can drink the elixir. To prevent his killer from seizing the potion, Chang E swallows it. She then floats to the moon and remains as a goddess.

In still another version, Yi is given the Palace of the Sun as a reward for shooting down the nine suns. But once each month, he ventures out to visit Chang E, the goddess who lives in the Palace of the Moon.

To create *Too Many Suns* I have combined elements of the different Yi myths. The Farm of Ten Brothers, however, is my own invention.